A lot can happen in 101-word tales.

Here are excerpts from three of them.

■

Jessica playfully kissed Dirk's ear
as she removed the .22 revolver from her purse.

Why didn't anyone ever tell the Dynamic Duo
that underwear goes *under* the tights?

✳

"—Or we'll get chain-sawed in our sleep,"
Jazmyne jumped in.

Turn the page and let the games begin.

FAST FICTION

VOLUME ONE

FAST FICTION

101 STORIES ◆ 101 WORDS EACH

SCOTTY CORNFIELD

Published by Flagstone Press.

www.scottycornfield.com

Cover & book design: Joe Sikoryak

Cover Photo: 21355537 / Book © Kitkana | Dreamstime.com

ISBN: 978-1-66786-632-1

Contents

Acknowledgements

Many people, spanning decades, have played a part in bringing this first book to life. I guess I have to start with Bob and Audrey Cornfield, who provided a lifetime of inspiration and encouragement as I meandered along my writing path.

Elvira Monroe, my high school journalism teacher, played an enormous role in teaching me how to write and, more importantly, introducing me to a craft I fell in love with.

I'd also like to thank my editor, Joyce Krieg; my designer, Joe Sikoryak; endorsers Tom Rosenstiel, Michael Latta and Anna Maria Manolo; my team of daily readers; my team of beta readers; and my Central Coast Writers small group (Mike and -et).

Finally, I need to thank my wife, Sandi, for her decades of support and patience through all of my adventures (including this latest one); Wes Leslie for his early prompt contributions; Charles Anderson for his brainstorming time; Susan Meyer for her incredible volume and variety of prompts that have inspired the bulk of these stories; and Scooter for his tolerance as I dictated ideas for stories while taking him on his early morning walks through the neighborhood. He almost never mocked me or barked when I came up with ridiculous ideas.

Dedication

A few years ago, I stumbled onto the *Monterey County Weekly*'s 101-Word Short Story Contest. Although I'd done a lot of other types of writing (screenplays, plays, newspaper and magazine articles/columns), writing fiction was an altogether different animal. When I read about the contest, I figured even I could probably string 101 words together in a way that made sense.

I wrote a few stories, entered the contest and, no surprise, I didn't do very well. Turns out, there's actually an art to telling a complete story (or at least something that feels complete) in only 101 words.

After entering the next year (and doing a bit better), I committed to write a story a day, every day. I missed a few days here and there but I eventually developed the discipline to write one every day.

Having written close to 400 stories as we go to press, I want to publicly acknowledge the *Monterey County Weekly* for helping me discover the world of Flash Fiction. It's a fascinating and challenging (at least to me) genre. Thank you, *Monterey County Weekly*, for your annual contest and your inspiration. I owe you far more than I could ever express in 101 words.

Foreword

This book is like writer's improv. Give me a prompt, I'll write the story. Initially, I have absolutely no idea where I'll take it, but after doing some mental gymnastics, I will come up with something. The key is that these stories only exist because of prompts provided by readers like you.

Want to play along? Send me your prompts: I'll write the story and you'll get a credit.

My inspiration for this book came from a contest in the local newspaper *(see Dedication, pg. xiii)*. I wrote it because everyone can find 45 seconds or so for some pleasure reading.

P.S. - The above foreword was written in 101 words. Go ahead and count. I'll wait.

PROMPT:

Found property

A Most Unexpected Gift

On the street, everybody knew him as "Shakes," but nobody knew where the name came from. A human hermit crab, he spent his days scavenging for whatever he could "find" be it from dumpsters, Wal-Marts or unlocked parked cars.

The keys he retrieved from a puddle in the alley were particularly intriguing because they belonged to a Mercedes. Not many cars like that around here. He kept pushing the horn button until he located his nearby prize.

He casually drove off like he owned the thing.

The real surprise would come later—when he discovered the body in the trunk.

PROMPT:

Keep them guessing

●

They Think They Know Us So Well

"What're you guys doing?" Taffy panted as she joined the other dogs at the dog park.

"Getting ready to play *Bend Over For Rover,* Duke answered.

"Can I play?" Taffy asked. "Wait. What's that?"

"We get our human's attention. We start sniffing around like we're gonna drop one and just when the human pulls out the poop bag and squats down, we move to another spot."

"My human brags about how he knows right when I'm about to go," Taffy said.

"That's what makes it so fun. We have them doing squats like they're at the gym. Humans—they're freakin' adorable."

PROMPT:
Surprise ending
of a sentence

I Know What You're Thinking

Sgt. "Stag" Stagnaro was one of the dumbest bosses ever. He talked slowly, used small words and you could usually guess where his sentences were going well before he reached the end of them.

He was like a human Mad Lib. If you ever interrupted him and completed the sentence, you were almost always right. Almost always.

After yesterday's narcotics raid, we were giving Stag the usual shit. His came back with, "Why don't you guys all go—"

"Fuck ourselves?" I interrupted.

"'Go home early' is what I was gonna say," Stag said.

Like I said, we were almost always right.

PROMPT:
Feather in his cap

The Nuances of
Family Connections

Everyone at the university knew there were only two likely candidates to fill the vacancy as department chair. Although not a prerequisite, Elizabeth recently earned a doctorate and she had published several articles. Drew, the other candidate, was an underachiever who was also the dean's nephew.

"They gave it to Elizabeth?" one startled teacher asked. "That's amazing."

"Agreed," another said. "Just when you think merit means nothing, this happens."

"I guess even the dean recognized that family connections alone can only take you so far."

"Elizabeth was clearly the best choice—even before her family donated the new five-story library."

PROMPT:
A word you've never
used in a story before

Mystery Within a Mystery

"Do you want to see where the bodies are?"

The CSI technician knelt down and snapped a photo. Her eyes stayed focused on the camera's display as she addressed homicide detectives Hunter and Pirrone.

"We got multiple bodies?" Hunter asked.

"It took us a while before we found the second one."

She led them down a fire-ravaged, water-soaked hallway.

"You might want to use a nose plug. It's redolent of the Blackthorne warehouse case."

Pirrone nodded, clearly lost. "Yeah, we agree."

Hunter whispered to his partner, "You have no idea what she's talking about, do you?"

"No fuckin' clue."

PROMPT:

Cruciverbalist

●

Where Else Will You Meet People Like This?

If you scored an invite to one of Hilary's parties, you were in for a treat. Eclectic guests were everywhere.

"Let me introduce you to someone." She led Philip and Barry to the bar.

"Philip, Barry, meet Wayne Manor."

"Wayne Manor? As in Batman's mansion?" Philip laughed.

"I'm a Batman historian. I even legally changed my name!"

Philip turned away. Mimicked a cuckoo clock chiming.

Barry elbowed him.

Turned to Wayne.

"As a lifetime Batman fan, I have so many questions. Let's start with an esoteric one—Why didn't anyone ever tell the Dynamic Duo that underwear goes *under* the tights?"

11

PROMPT:
*To make a
long story short*

Keeping the Story Straight

Handcuffed in the back of the police car, Arturo, Beto and Billy whispered.

"If we got our story tight and everybody puts it out right, they got nothing," said Arturo.

"Keep it tight," Beto seconded.

"So what's the story?" Billy asked.

"We took the 22 bus to the mall. Kicked it for a while. Went to the food court. Got a large pepperoni pizza. Split it. Hopped the 22 back when they grabbed us."

"Cool," Billy nodded. "We got this."

The car door opened and a large cop pulled Billy from the car.

"We did it, officer. All three of us."

PROMPT:

Workplace drama

Surgically Removed

"Removing the gall bladder," Dr. Enders casually announced to the rest of the surgical team.

"We're not waiting for lab results?" Nurse Sinclair asked.

"No," he glared.

"If it's functioning normally, why not—"

"Come back after med school, a residency and 15 years of experience—then we can discuss it."

"Reckless body snatcher," Sinclair muttered.

"What was that?" Enders thrust a scalpel inches from her throat.

She jerked back.

"What is wrong with—

"Stabile questioned my work too. She's now the only unemployable nurse in California."

Wide-eyed, Sinclair froze.

"Cut!" the director yelled.

"Awesome!" he clapped. "Break for lunch, everybody."

PROMPT:
Finger Pick

Model Behavior

People never believe me when I tell them I'm a model. "You can't be," they'll say. "You're not tall enough —or anorexic."

It doesn't get any easier when they learn I'm a hand model. "That's not a thing," is the typical response. This usually leads to me trying to prove to them that it is, indeed "a thing."

Tonight is no exception. This guy at the bar thinks he's scoring points with every stupid joke he makes about "hand jobs."

Unfortunately for him, last week I did a print ad for Smith & Wesson. They let me keep the product.

Big mistake.

PROMPT:

Everything changes

●

Verbal Judo at the Breakfast Table

Danny finished his cereal. "I hope we get pizza at school again today."

"Yesterday was pizza. Today it'll be something else," his mom replied. "It always changes."

As raindrops pelted the kitchen window, Danny posed another question. "Why's it have to rain today? Yesterday we got to play outside."

"Take a guess."

"Because everything changes," Danny mocked.

He pushed away his empty cereal bowl. Flashed his version of an irresistible smile. "If I ask nice, can I PLEASE have a cookie?"

"Every morning you ask. Every morning my answer's the same, right?"

"But you said 'everything changes'"?

"Go ask your father."

PROMPT:

Unpredictable

She Should've Invested
in a Security Camera

Gene's so far above me intellectually that I'll never understand how we're best friends. He has degrees in things I've never heard of, yet here we are, on another of his incongruous adventures.

We're inside one of those sketchy psychic houses. You know the ones—they look like franchises, and Madame Zelda is bestowing Gene with all kinds of vague truths about him, while he (an actual Mensa member!) is eating it up.

The door bursts open and three men in bright windbreakers labeled "police" enter, yelling "search warrant!"

We're all thinking the same thing: the psychic didn't see this coming?

PROMPT:
Duplicity

Reading Between the Lies

They had both been married multiple times, though not to each other. The timing had never been right for them. Instead, they told countless lies to their respective partners, keeping their sporadic affair going throughout the decades.

He stood next to her hospital bed, taking in her cancer-ravaged body.

"You don't look so bad," he lied.

She barely lifted her bruised arm.

"Hope not. I feel pretty good," she returned the fib.

"When they let you out of here, we should…" He turned away as his voice cracked.

"Yeah," she said softly. "That sounds nice."

Her eyelids fluttered. Alarms sounded.

PROMPT:

Fake Gucci

No Right Answer

Inside the airport's international terminal, the customs inspector scanned the nervous passenger's declaration.

"Doesn't look like you claimed that brand-new Rolex you're wearing," the inspector noted.

"Oh, uh, I got that before the trip," Melvin stuttered.

"If I find the receipt on you, you'll pay triple the duty. On a $10,000 watch, that's gonna be pricy."

"It's fake," Melvin said. "Total knock-off. I paid fifty for it."

The inspector smiled. "I appreciate your honesty. And here I thought you were trying to smuggle an expensive watch."

Melvin relaxed.

"Instead, you're only guilty of a trademark violation. Nice work, kid."

PROMPT:

Immutable

What It Takes to Change a Man

The senior senator was, like Mt. Rushmore, a permanent fixture whom his constituents had counted on for decades. They always knew where he stood, and, for the most part, they stood right with him. He was a proud, evangelical Christian. In his dream world, this meant no gay teachers, no laws prohibiting discrimination against gays and of course, only heterosexual marriages should be legal. His voting record always reflected his views.

Then his son came home from college and broke the unimaginable news: the proud senator's namesake came out to his parents. He was a closeted Democrat.

His father disowned him.

PROMPT:

Justification

Small Talk in the Waiting Room

"So you actually do that for a living?" I tried to sound casual but failed miserably. If he was telling me the truth, he was some kind of mafia dude.

He gave a "whaddaya-gonna-do?" silent reply. It made sense.

A seedy bar in Queens is where we should've been (instead of our dentist's office in Brooklyn).

"Do you feel bad about your victims?" I treaded lightly.

Another shrug. "They usually owe money. They're not bad people—they just make bad decisions. I help them."

"Oh," I said relieved. "You're not a killer."

"Of course not," he assured.

"Almost never."

PROMPT:
Holiday

The Gift of Mercy

Jae and Anita Benson weren't typical residents of Villosa Canyon for at least three reasons: First, while the town was upper middle-class, they were billionaires. Second, they were Black (it was a very white town). Finally, they were ridiculously friendly—meet them once and you were friends for life.

Right before Christmas, their $50,000 holiday decorations were destroyed by underprivileged, out-of-town kids who randomly picked their victim. City officials immediately competed to see who could be tougher on the juveniles' parents who received $10,000 fines.

When the Bensons learned about the punishment, they anonymously paid the fines. Naturally.

PROMPT:

Hot pretzels

Maybe Tomorrow

There was an excellent chance that he was going to snap today—like CNN, breaking news mass shooter snap. He fit the profile. Everything in his past had led him here: broken home; childhood beatings; bullied at school; raised by alcoholic mother.

Locked in his bedroom, he seethed as he re-read his termination papers from the factory. The assault rifle in the corner beckoned him when his mother used her key to enter. His jaw tightened.

"Who's ready for his favorite treat?" She set down a dish of homemade pretzels.

He grinned and the hatred instantly vanished…for the moment.

PROMPT:
Bicycle

Thank You for Your (non) Service

"Why can't you take my order? I waited in line like everyone else."

I was on my bike speaking into the crappy speaker system at the drive-through window of a fast-food restaurant I won't name for fear of being sued. Let's just say they are now my "arch" nemesis.

"Sorry, sir. The rules say no pedestrians or bicycles."

I got off my bike and did the walk of shame to the car behind me.

"This is stupid," I said, "but would you mind ordering a Big Mac and McFlurry for me?"

I guess I suck at keeping secrets, huh?

PROMPT:
A hobby

Honesty Should Count for Something

Kenneth sat at his assigned table in the middle of the gym. He readjusted his name tag again and waited as the next speed-date candidate strode up to him. She's done this before. Way too cocky.

She sat across from him. Locked in on his name tag.

She thrust out her hand. "Maggie May. What do you do for fun, Kenneth?"

He leaned in close. Whispered, "I break into houses and steal ladies' underwear."

Maggie laughed loud enough to turn heads.

"Nice," she said. "Finally, an original opening line."

Kenneth just nodded.

Can't say I didn't warn her, he thought.

PROMPT:

*There's always
tomorrow*

Nobody Knows for Sure

The expression "the third time's the charm" didn't apply to Adam. He'd beaten cancer twice, but now, as he waited for his test results, he was certain he knew.

What he did find surprising were the weird places his mind went. Bizarre thoughts like "Why did I commit to a full year of that premium cable package?" and, "Will people freak out if I have my memorial while I'm still around to see it?"

And then something truly unexpected happened—a complete paradigm shift.

He booked that dream vacation. He dated above his level.

He saw his future.

It was now.

PROMPT:

Bargain

I'm a Good Neighbor

She has fuckin' balls. I'll give her that. Her husband's been dead a week and she's having her own estate sale. The garage-sale vultures circle her driveway—fully expecting to be dealing with a neutral third party. Instead, they've got the new widow who, by the way, seems to be taking it all rather well. She should. She killed him and I'm pretty sure nobody but me knows it—certainly not the cops who wrote it off as a random hit-and-run.

I wave her over. Smile as I whisper, "I know."

Who knew garage sales were this entertaining?

PROMPT:

Sudden stop

■

Falling in Love Can Really Hurt

Gabe and Sonia were a happy couple who did everything together. They sold dope, ran numbers and traded in stolen property together.

They would've worked out together, but they weighed over 300 pounds each. Eating was more their hobby.

When the cops raided their third-story apartment, Sonia jumped out the window. Gabe followed, landing on top of her.

During the hospital interrogation, Gabe said, "When I saw Sonia lying there, I figured if I landed on her, it wouldn't hurt me."

"What about what it would do to her?" the cop asked.

"Didn't have time to think about that part."

PROMPT:

Esemplastic

●

A Leader Who Knew How to Talk the Talk

She had been a city council person, a union leader and a county supervisor, and then Amanda set her sights on mayor. She succeeded because she was a legitimate problem-solver supported by Democrats and Republicans alike. The combined appeal made her hard to beat.

Cindy, her campaign manager, made sure every speech, sign and news release mentioned Amanda's savvy at bringing people together. "The Great Unifier," was her nickname.

"After the Republican business lunch, we have the fire fighters' union and Hispanic Chamber of Commerce," Cindy said. "What's the Great Unifier have planned for tonight?"

"I'm seeing a divorce lawyer."

PROMPT:

A thorn in the paw

Law of the Jungle

I was taking the trash out behind my apartment when I spotted JR. The vicious gang member was blood-soaked. His broken arm was pinned underneath the dumpster. I thought about ignoring the neighborhood terrorist's silent plea. Instead, I managed to roll the dumpster enough to free him.

He walked off. No gratitude.

Two weeks later as I walked down our dark alley, the gang began following me. When they caught up, one spun me around. I raised my hands, ready to hand over my wallet.

JR's eyes met mine. "Wrong guy," was all he said.

I finally got my thanks.

PROMPT:
Sloth

He Made Work a Four-Letter Word

After embracing sloth as his sin of choice, Stu barely graduated from his Catholic high school, but that was only the beginning of his love for the sin of the unambitious.

Upon graduation, Stu's new focus was on finding a way to live while still embodying a world view of laziness and inertia.

He landed a menial office job and became an instant legend. "He's taken unproductivity to genius levels," co-workers marveled.

His famous "lazy-cations," where he'd spend a solid week on his couch, were legendary.

If he'd just gotten up when he first smelled smoke, he might've survived.

PROMPT:

Touchstones of our character

Nobody Said There'd be a Test

From day one at the police academy, Ernie and Gil became fast friends who did everything together.

They leaned over a table in the police training unit, filling out applications for a new fitness program.

Ernie pointed at a large box of donuts nearby.

"Think that one's filled with custard?"

Gil shrugged. "Bite it and see."

"I should eat healthier. That apple fritter's mostly fruit, right?"

He snatched it and took a massive bite. Flashed a thumbs up as Gil devoured a glazed donut.

The fitness instructor approached. "There's a test to get into our program. You two just ate yours."

PROMPT:
One-way ticket

Guess I Missed the Memo

I pull to the departures curb without asking which airline she wants—does she even know?

There was no break up—not even a "we need time apart" thing, so I'm playing catch up here.

"Where you going?"

"I don't know."

"For how long?"

She just shrugs.

When she opens the door to leave, I see she only has a small backpack.

Significant?

Before I can analyze, she drops a quick "thanks."

As she enters the terminal, she studies each airline counter.

The cops shoo me along and I pull away, straining to see which airline she picks.

I'll never know.

PROMPT:
*Pondering the complete
absence of...*

Lessons Learned Inside the Crime Scene Tape

Chewing an unlit cigar, Cooper strolled the crime scene. Expressionless, he checked off boxes in his head: unidentified body in parking lot; no witnesses; no physical evidence; no obvious cause of death.

"What do you call this again?" Davis, the new kid in Homicide, asked.

"Body from the sky," Cooper grunted.

"Maybe the uniforms'll find a witness."

Cooper laughed. "Nobody saw nothing and if they did, they didn't."

"How long 'til we get DNA results?"

"Months. In-custody cases get priority."

"If somebody's locked up already, they got their case. We need DNA to find *our* killer."

"Welcome to Homicide, kid."

PROMPT:

Wrongful conviction

Even Lawyers Have Appeal

In another era, the kids would've played "Cops and Robbers," but next-door neighbors Chance and Rico, influenced by their single parents, played "Court" in the driveway.

Since his dad was a public defender, Chance defended clients and argued for "de-funning the police." Rico adopted his mom's D.A. role, cautioning against the "slippy slope" Chance was creating.

During one debate, shouts of "lethal rejection" and "rehabilitizing my client" drew the parents out of each house to investigate.

"Totally my fault," Chance's dad said. "Don't be silly," Rico's mom countered.

They shared smiles.

Six month later, justice became "just us."

PROMPT:
"People who live in brick bars
should not know Stones"

■

Where Sensitivity Training Goes to Die

Fragile egos were a fatal flaw for those in the Robbery Homicide Division, where the ability to hurl brutal insults was right up there with converting oxygen to CO2.

Danny, recognized as the master of witty verbal abuse, always walked the line when it came to the slurs he dished out.

"Hey, Brad," he told the nerdy detective who had just transferred in from Computer Crimes. "Necrophelia is contagious up here, so beware."

"Your wife said she experienced it on your honeymoon," Brad nonchalantly replied.

Jaws dropped. Everyone froze.

"Welcome to the unit," Danny fake-smiled. Then, under his breath, "Asshole."

PROMPT:
*Profound lack of
pleasure*

Too Lost to Know It

He had zoned out in front of his computer when a text from Maddie broke his trance. Dave blinked and read it.

"Just sent u a quiz. Only 10 questions. Take it."

"About what?" he asked.

"Depression."

When he didn't reply, Maddie followed up.

"U used to like going to movies, concerts, kayaking, hanging with us after work…"

"Just bored," he texted.

"Take it."

He had only answered the second question when he inexplicably felt his eyes well up with tears.

He needed fixing. The sudden discovery, though painful, felt… good.

Good was something he hadn't felt in a long time.

PROMPT:
*Being possessed by
something...unnatural*

He'll Never Be Completely Alone

He'd heard the voices ever since he could remember. When he was small, his parents and the other adults encouraged him. "You've got a great imagination," they'd say. "Never lose that."

But by middle school, he saw the discomfort in their faces if he mentioned obeying the voices. He learned to stop sharing.

Now a high school senior, the voices were louder than ever and their demands were more complex.

He desperately wanted to tell his parents, but he wouldn't dare say anything that would ruin tonight's special event—their anniversary.

Tomorrow would be better.

Unfortunately, they'd be dead by then.

PROMPT:

*Man-eating
vulture bees*

●

Pushing the Envelope
Until the Envelope Pushes Back

Known as the Daredevil Duo, twins Bryce and Taylor lived to out-do each other when it came to death-defying stunts. Occasionally, they even teamed up to cheat death.

Today's adrenaline rush was a skydiving stunt where they planned to switch chutes with each other while free-falling. The action would be filmed for reality TV.

Despite a total lack of preparation, the twins pulled it off, barely walking away.

Their celebration abruptly ended when younger brother Junior, doing a hand stand on a speeding motorcycle, crashed into them.

Just like that, Junior drained the gene pool.

PROMPT:
Plausible deniability

What You Don't Know, Can't Hurt You

Vincent, feet up on his desk, puffed on his cigar.

"You took care of it."

The two goons stood in front of the desk. They nodded together.

"It's done," one finally said. "That's all you wanted to know, you said."

"Right, but is it done permanently or could it be a problem later?"

"The first one."

Vincent hesitated. "And the body?"

"So you do want to know," the thug said.

Vincent beckoned him to continue.

"We cracked his melon with a hammer. Chopped him up and tossed him into the bay in three different places. What else don't you wanna know?"

PROMPT:
Robocall

He Should've Bought the Warranty

For the past three days, he'd received the same robocall advising him that his car warranty was about to expire. Blocking the number hadn't worked. On day three, just before he hit the disconnect button, he thought he heard the recording use his first name. Impossible, he thought.

An avalanche of similar emails followed. Then, at two a.m., a text woke him up—another car warranty pitch.

Enraged, he ran outside, shoved paper into his gas tank and ignited it.

As the fire department doused his smoldering car, another text hit his phone. "Your home warranty is about to expire."

PROMPT:
*There's no place
like home*

When Being Nice Isn't Enough

When the cold front finally struck, Jimmy, a small-time, often homeless criminal, wasn't prepared.

Thompson, with the patrol car heater blasting away, rolled down the window when Jimmy flagged him down.

"Take me in, Thompson," Jimmy said.

"Can't do it, Jimmy. You didn't do anything."

"I'm drunk in public." He pretended to sway.

"You need to be at the shelter."

Jimmy frowned. "All full up."

"Stay warm if you can, man." Thompson pulled away.

A large rock cracked the police car's window.

Jimmy ran up to the car. Turned around and put his hands behind his back.

"How about now?"

PROMPT:

Grim Reaper

●

Lessons from a Grim Reaper

The black-robed reapers assembled in the cave.

"Where is he?" the leader looked around.

"Sorry I'm late, guys." Denny bounced in, sporting his glitter-bedazzled scythe.

"So it is true," the leader said. "You're rebranding death."

"He's calling himself the 'Grin Greeter," one shouted.

"His Instagram is blowing up," another complained.

"The whole grim thing worked for eons, fellas, but It's 2022. I listen to them. We laugh and they willingly come along."

"But they don't fear you," the leader said.

"Nope, and I have the top delivery time here."

"Shit," the leader conceded. "He may be on to something."

PROMPT:
Train

Is This Why
I Still Commute by Train?

"This is a robbery! Reach for it."

I peek over my newspaper and a guy is waving around what I'm guessing is a fake gun.

Before I can digest what's happening, a squeaky voice from the other end of the car yells, "Yeah, what Jerry said!" He's swinging nunchucks. One of them flies off the rope and cracks a window.

So far, Butch and Sumdunce aren't real impressive.

Butch yells, "No names, Avery!" As he runs toward Sumdunce/ Avery, I trip him. His toy gun shatters.

For the umpteenth time, I swear off taking the train. Back to reading my newspaper.

PROMPT:

A dream coming true

How to Break the News

Dr. Cohen, her oncologist, had just given her the good news she had hoped was coming. Audra sagged with relief.

"Hello….anybody home?" Audra looked up. Monica, the medical assistant, had just jarred Audra out of a powerful day dream. Dr. Cohen was nowhere in sight.

"Oh, sorry." Audra blinked.

Monica smiled and winked. "The doctor is ready for you."

Audra steeled her nerves, nodded and rose.

Monica opened the door to Dr. Cohen's office. The entire staff was inside. Party hats and helium balloons.

"Glad you could join us for your *last* visit," Dr. Cohen beamed.

"We'll all miss you."

PROMPT:
"Where does this lead?"
"Nowhere good."

It's Always Funny
Until Somebody Gets Blown Up

Ever since Chip and I became partners in the ECU (Explosives Control Unit), we've had a routine. One of us points to a wire on the suspected bomb and asks the other, "You cool if I cut this?" The response is something like, "Yeah, but let's see where it goes first."

It's a joke because, of course, we cut nothing until we know exactly where it goes. We interrupt one circuit and boom—game over. Leave the "red or the blue wire?" stuff to Tom Cruise.

In our world, all wires go nowhere good until proven otherwise.

That part's no joke.

PROMPT:
Spiritual lard

●

Some People Are Just Good

Reverend Dickerson added more weights to the leg press machine at the exclusive gym. As he climbed in, Beth approached.

"Hey, Reverend, mind if I ask you a question?"

"Shoot."

"I see your sermons on TV and it seems like you never stop working. Why do you do it?"

"It's transactional. I give them guidance, hope, answers. At least I try to."

"And what do you get?" Beth asked.

"The gift of helping others, of sharing what I've learned, of making a better world."

"That sounds fair."

"And of course there's the yacht, the vacation homes, the plane. I do OK."

PROMPT:

Seminal work

●

America's Own Michelangelo

For today's educational moment, we pay tribute to Dr. Samuel Francis, the inventor of the spork. Samuel—we call him by his first name just to make him appear less god-like—did not coin the term "spork" but he did invent the seriously underrated utensil.

Interestingly enough, 300 years before Samuel's invention, there existed a fork on one end with a spoon on the other. This became known as a "sucket." Please—don't go there.

Samuel also invented a cane with a hidden compartment for bus fare.

If you fail to see the genius in that, feel free to sucket.

PROMPT:

Zeitgeist

Hangin' with My Time Traveler

Everybody needs at least one friend who is—what's the right word? Unique. For me, it's Mick. He says things like "groovy" and "far out"—and not in an even slightly ironic way.

He hops out of his '68 Mustang, wearing bell bottoms and a tie-dyed shirt.

"Dig this," Mick shows me his peace sign choker.

"You're late," I tell him, "by about forty years."

"Mellow out. You sound like The Man."

I laugh. Whatever influenced him was powerful.

We climb into my Tesla. I scroll through my phone and fire up the soundtrack to Woodstock.

Totally random choice, right?

PROMPT:
Dig two graves

■

Purely a Business Transfer

In the world of organized crime, Moe and Gio were bottom feeders. Limited by their room-temperature I.Q.s, they were accustomed to menial tasks.

Digging side-by-side graves, they took a quick break.

"I'm gonna be happy when the bosses figure out how valuable we are," Moe said.

"I think it's gonna be real soon," Gio added. "Ozzie said, 'Dig these graves like your best work ever and I promise things will be looking up after this.'"

"And I heard him tell the other bosses we wouldn't be burying any more stiffs."

"Maybe we really are going places."

PROMPT:

Home repair

Beyond Repair

She was on her back, under the kitchen sink.

"Can I get the wrench?"

He bent over the toolbox, grabbed a wrench and dropped it into her waiting hand.

"You don't need to do this," he said.

"Just let me try."

"I'm talking about another 'girls weekend,'" he replied.

"I need it," echoed from under the sink. "When I get back, we can talk about the—"

"—I don't think so," he countered. "You can't fix it. Not this time."

She slid out to face him.

"You're not talking about the sink."

They locked eyes.

"I'm moving on. It's what people do."

PROMPT:
Disinformation

Teddy's Moment of Regret

On the drive to jail, Teddy's monologue from the back of the police car consisted of "I ain't no snitch," "I wouldn't tell you shit even if I knew anything," and "Watch your backs. I'm coming for both of you."

The two cops chauffeuring Teddy laughed. "You as scared as I am?" Pancho asked Cisco. "Even more," Cisco answered.

As they walked Teddy past the inmates, Pancho said, "We got your back, Teddy. Just call if you need us."

Horrified, Teddy looked at the cons. "The fucker's lying!"

The cops shared a private grin. Teddy was in for a long night.

PROMPT:

Consigliere

●

Reality Check

Although his office was only on the fourth floor, Don Romano enjoyed the view that overlooked downtown and the university.

"How can I help this time?" he asked Tony.

"I come to you, Don Romano, seeking your wise counsel, as I have done many times before."

"You have. Also, please call me Dr. Romano—using my full name is… disturbing."

"I call you 'Don' out of respect, as my father and my family have done for years."

"Whatever. Need advice? As your academic advisor, I'm telling you to stop watching mob movies and start going to class. Now get out, capeesh?"

PROMPT:

*An ending that
doesn't end*

●

Compromising Positions

Frank marched into the kitchen, suitcase in hand. "I'm leaving."

"Uh huh." Lisa, undismayed, emptied the dishwasher.

"I mean it this time. Soon as I grab my stuff."

"Right. Need any help?"

"You don't believe me?" he challenged her.

She made eye contact. "There's no makeup sex, if that's what you're after."

"What if I finally move the Chevy off the lawn?"

"Only if you get rid of the boat too."

"Absolutely not. The boat's a deal-breaker."

"Oh well," she turned away.

"Shit," he exhaled. "I'll have to fix the trailer first."

"Don't get too worn out," she smiled playfully.

PROMPT:

Miasma

She Bought a Ticket
but Didn't Like the Show

Inside the crime scene tape protecting the home's front yard, a woman, clipboard in hand, vomited into a bed of roses.

"Who's that and why is she puking on your scene?"

"That, Lieutenant Mendez, is one of the county's finest grand jury members," Detective Rhodes cheerfully answered. "They're auditing Homicide this week."

"Lucky you. So why's she puking?"

"We may have told her the best way to manage the smell of a ripe one is to breathe deeply through the nose—filter out the bad stuff."

"She believed you?"

"The proof's in the pudding."

The woman wretched again.

"Lots of pudding."

PROMPT:
Delphic

Just a Lucky Guess?

As they walked away from the fortune teller, Margy, dumbfounded, turned toward Emily.

"I know you're a skeptic but did she nail me or what?"

"I'd go with 'or what.'"

"But she knew about a change in my relationship."

"She saw the tan line now that you don't wear your wedding ring."

"Maybe. I do like stability. She knew that."

"She also said you're seeking a change. Everything just vague enough to apply."

Margy shrugged. "Wasn't that weird when she said something about your health as we were leaving?"

Emily turned serious. "Um, let's sit. I got something to tell you."

PROMPT:

Onomatopoeia

●

Why I Don't Need to Watch TV

He's like the human version of a cartoon character, which is why hanging around Jackie is never boring.

Completely unrelated to whatever subject we were discussing, he says, "I wanna replace that thing—waddaya call it—that's behind the door to stop it?"

"A door stop."

"Right. Scooter thinks it's a toy. Boing, boing. He loves playing with it."

"Then someone rings the doorbell. Ya know, ding, and he goes nuts."

"And don't even get me started about the meows of the neighbor's cat."

"You taking another sound effects class?"

"Shhhh!"

That's Jackie. Always needing to get in the final sound.

PROMPT:

Dystopia of crabbiness

●

Even Love Children Have Limits

Being the last of the Baby Boomers, Sunshine and her soulmate, Ziggy, always bemoaned the fact that they missed out on the communes and utopian societies.

Now retired, they moved to a lakeside mountain community where they established the kind of place they'd always envisioned. They invited like-minded friends to join them and soon Bliss Farm was born.

Everyone's mellow evaporated when Harmony and Buzz moved in. Their "bad vibes" led to being banished, forcing them to set up camp across the lake. Soon, other Bliss rejects joined them, and thus, Bummer Bluff, a haven for the "uncool" was founded.

PROMPT:

Truce

●

Domestic Terrierist

It was a recipe for disaster and Quentin knew it the day his wife brought home Bosco, a rescue pup from the shelter. Bosco was a mutt of undetermined origin but one thing was clear—he loved to feast on new plants, drip irrigation systems and outdoor lighting wires.

After unsuccessfully trying every solution short of returning Bosco, Quentin gave up. He spread cheap plants and irrigation hose within easy reach around the yard. Bosco quickly devoured two plants and some hose line before growing bored. Once it was clear that Quentin had surrendered, so did Bosco.

The war was over.

PROMPT:

*Throw yourself at the
ground and miss*

■

Oh, Henry!

To call Henry and Roseanne "simple-minded" would be generous. Their lack of intellect was only topped by their ineptitude in pretty much everything.

Their decision to park in the worst part of town was a classic example.

"Please don't take the ring my wife hides in her purse," Henry pleaded.

After taking their money and the ring, the robber gave them five seconds to leave before he'd start shooting.

Henry threw the car into gear and peeled out. The gear turned out to be reverse.

Henry said killing the robber was accidental.

After investigating Henry, the cops absolutely believed him.

PROMPT:

Paracusia

Trust Me:
It Sounds Better than It Is

I'm not a mind reader, per se, but I do hear other people's thoughts. Not all of them, fortunately. That would be torturous.

From time to time I contemplate what to do with this ability. For a second, I even considered being a professional poker player or something, but that's not really me.

You'd think having access to information like this would be life-changing, but sometimes—lots of times, actually—you're better off not knowing. If I could turn it off, at least occasionally, I would.

Like right now. I know exactly what you're thinking about me.

You're probably right.

PROMPT:

One Mississippi

●

A Rush to Judgement

While their parents picnicked nearby, the kids played football.

One kid shouted "One Mississippi, Two Mississippi, Three Mississippi," before rushing the quarterback.

"Hold on," Harvey yelled, stopping the game.

"Mississippi? Really? Don't you kids know their civil rights record?"

Billy, the quarterback said, "Fine. We'll do 'One alligator' instead."

"And encourage slaughtering reptiles just to make wallets?" one mom added.

"One rigatoni?" Billy offered.

"Why ridicule the gluten-intolerant?" another parent asked.

Billy and the kids headed to the playground.

"Good idea," Harvey said. "Play on the monkey bars."

Billy spun around, shocked.

"Don't you mean primate ladder? Who raised you?"

PROMPT:
Sorry

Tonight's Menu: Carrots and Sticks

The sign on the door say ""Interrogation Room," but we call it our happy place. Right now I'm watching my partner, Mikey, work. It's a thing of beauty.

He's one of the nicest humans on the planet, but…he can also snap like a twig if provoked. It just happened, so now he's disparaging the suspect's mother until even this stone-cold killer cries big time. Next, Mikey'll shift gears and apologize. He'll do the classic good cop/bad cop routine—all by himself.

Mikey hugs it out with the perp. Naturally, he confesses.

It's the circle of life—without parole.

PROMPT:
The impossible has
a kind of integrity
that the merely
improbable lacks.

●

The Ultimate Challenge

Like most small children, Devin Franklin went through a phase where he did not like to be told "no." But unlike others, he never outgrew it. He wasn't spoiled or entitled. He just reacted differently to being told that he couldn't do something. It became an obsession.

Now a famous inventor known for creating products he was told were impossible, Devin was appearing on every news-making show, clamoring to hear about his groundbreaking jetpack.

As he approached the busy street corner near the TV studio, the pedestrian sign flashed "Don't Walk."

Even his obituary could not resist highlighting the irony.

PROMPT:

Trillions

●

Going with the Flow

"Where you off to?" I asked Barkley.

"I dunno," he shrugged. "I got nowhere special to be so I thought I'd just go with the flow and see where I wind up."

That was *so* Barkley. I've never known anyone who put less stock in making plans, and yet things always seemed to work out for him. At least I'd never seen him hurting for anything.

While I admit that I like a bit more structure than my aimless drifter buddy, truth be told, I have no more control over my existence than he does.

"Why's that?" you ask.

We're plankton.

PROMPT:

Plumber's crack

●

Equal Opportunity Employers

"You're finally working on the leak?" Laura asked, entering the kitchen.

Dave rose from under the sink.

"Even better. The plumber just left and guess what? No more leaks."

Later, at the neighborhood picnic, the men chatted around the barbecue.

"I heard Phil worked on your sink. How's my favorite plumber's crack?"

"Wide open for business," Dave smiled.

"I got an appointment scheduled for Tuesday. Looking forward to the view."

Laura marched up and glared at Dave.

"That plumber you guys all talk about—Phil…is a woman?"

"Uh, I guess."

The men scattered.

Laura smirked. "It all makes sense now."

PROMPT:

Run silent, run deep

Tommy's Rude Awakening

Tommy wasn't your typical drug kingpin. He was smart, successful and extraordinarily careful. His house was a fortress, designed to keep out cops—or anyone else after his dope.

So when he awoke to find a host of DEA task force weapons aimed at him, Tommy was confused.

"How'd you get past the fence?"

"Used bolt cutters last night," one agent said.

"And the cameras and alarms?"

"Killed the power."

"I never heard the door busted down."

"Someone gave us a key."

"Damn. You guys are good."

"So were you, Tommy."

"You're making it sound like it's all over."

It was.

PROMPT:

Bell, mowing grass

●

Meet-Cut at the Garden Show

Courtney, exiting the garden show, paused as Ben leapt from the riding mower and ended his lawn-cutting demo with a flourish.

"Interested in a mower?" Ben asked.

"Not in this lifetime," Courtney answered, taking in his bell bottoms.

"I'm Ben. Guess you don't look like the tractor type."

"Based on those fancy pants you're rockin', you don't look like the fashion type."

He laughed. "Touché. They lost my luggage. All I found was a thrift store on the way here."

"If they sold time machines, you'd have been set."

Ben grinned. "You got a name?"

"I'm still deciding," she smiled.

PROMPT:

Fish-out-of-water

●

Teaching Immigrants About America

Although the English transplant had lived in Oakland for two years now, Julie still felt like she was on an extended holiday. Today she was at the Giants game on a double date with three co-workers.

Jake sat next to her and patiently explained it all.

"The guy standing on the big dusty tosses the cow melon to the smacker," Jake explained.

Bruce, his co-worker, guffawed and spit out his beer—again.

"Is this when we jump up and yell 'Flip the muffin?" Julie asked Jake.

"Not yet."

"I can't wait for you to show her hockey," Bruce said.

PROMPT:
*The noose of men and
dogs is tightening now*

Work with What You Got

"I want a tight perimeter. This asshole's not getting away."

Sergeant Billings circled the target house on his map.

He grabbed his radio. "I need a canine for a barricaded suspect."

"None available," dispatch advised.

"Can I help, Sarge?" Holt offered. "I can—"

"You'll have to do. After I announce you, give him a few barks and some heavy door clawing.

With Holt set, Billings yelled, "Come out or we send in the dogs!"

Holt's realistic growls and scratching flushed the suspect out.

Holt cuffed him, ran to a tree and urinated.

Billings stared, dumbfounded. "Is he actually marking his territory?"

PROMPT:

Orbisculate

●

Must We Share Everything?

Hanging with my friend Marcus is always entertaining, mostly because the man's brain never stops. Plus, he shares his thoughts—in real time.

We're in line, waiting to get into the new buffet in town. "Look at that girl's shorts," Marcus points out at the word "juicy" stenciled across the back. "Do we need to know this?" he ponders.

Now his eyes move to what appears to be an entire traveling soccer team. They're wearing matching sweats labeled "Hungary."

Marcus snaps. "Does everyone have to share everything? We know you're hungry. You're at a buffet!"

Irony, meet my good friend Marcus.

PROMPT:

Candle wax

●

Counterintuitive

He awoke to the delicious aroma of his wife's homemade muffins.

His mouth watered as he got out of bed and sauntered into the kitchen.

The cluttered, center island countertop resembled a science lab.

His wife slid a lit candle toward him.

"Smell my new blueberry coffee cake candle."

"This is what I was smelling?"

She nodded, beaming.

"I can't eat this," he muttered.

"Why would you want to eat a candle?"

"Why would you take the time to make something that smells this good that you can't eat?"

"Because I can sell these next Christmas."

"Not to men, you can't."

PROMPT:

Two pyromaniacs

When Sparks Fly

Standing near the front of the crowd, Manfred was deeply engrossed, watching the warehouse burn.

He turned around when someone bumped him.

"Sorry," Lexi said as she slid up next to him. "Every time I get a good view, somebody moves."

The excitement on her face was unlike anything he'd seen from his other fire crowds. He was instantly intrigued.

"What do you think?" he asked cautiously.

"It's a tragedy," she said through just a hint of a smile.

"Yeah," he agreed. "And yet…"

"Wanna get out of here?" she whispered breathlessly.

He grinned. Had he finally found a kindred spirit?

PROMPT:
Delphic

My Next Door Stranger

It took years before I finally accepted the fact that Bob (if that was even his real name) was someone I would never really know.

The adventure began when he moved next door. "Where you coming from?," I asked. "You know. Here and there," was his opening salvo. His ambiguities ranged from the elementary ("My favorite color? Plaid") to the exasperating ("Ever married? Well, I always sought happiness.").

After Bob died, his brother Jim enlightened me. "Bob had a pathological fear of direct answers."

At least that's what Jim said before he returned to where he said he lived ("Rural America").

PROMPT:

Denouement

■

Some Parents Are
More Clueless than Others

"I heard you got grounded for throwing the party? How'd they catch you?" Linnae asked Derek.

"They said it didn't look right when they came home."

"No way. Your place was clean when we left."

"They said it was 'too clean.' My mom noticed vacuum tracks."

"I thought we totally nailed it when we took the trash to the dump and brought back somebody else's garbage."

"Me too, but my dad said something about the garbage bag strings being a different color."

"He caught that shit? Damn. Your mom's a cop and your dad's a detective. Sucks to be you, dude."

PROMPT:

Urgent emptiness

What Do You Do If You Get There?

For as long as she could remember, Mary Beth knew what she wanted to do with her life. She needed to cure cancer. She was specifically focused, obsessed really, on curing Retinoblastoma, the disease that had stolen her mother's vision, and since it was hereditary, well, it hit a bit too close to home.

After 31 years of setbacks, toiling in obscurity, Mary Beth discovered the cure, won a Nobel Prize and became medicine's equivalent of a rock star.

As she was flying back from Stockholm with her prize, the panic set in.

She had vanquished her lifelong enemy.

Now what?

PROMPT:

Kindergarten protocol

He Makes a Good Case
for Reincarnation

"What I do this time?" Jacob studied the principal's inspirational posters.

"Classmates say you're not exercising good citizenship," Mrs. Reichert replied.

Jacob shrugged. "It's jump rope. If you can't afford to lose, don't play."

"What do you mean by afford?"

Jacob locked eyes with her.

"Jacob?"

"It's Jake. And if you wanna talk more, I want somebody here."

Mrs. Reichert laughed. "Like who—your lawyer?"

"Like Danny….Danny Lewis. Sixth grade."

The principal's eyes widen.

"The kid who flunked four times?"

"Hey—you got your role models. I got mine."

Jake sauntered out.

This can't be his first life, she thought.

PROMPT:

A close shave

●

A Saturday Ritual Goes Awry

He was seventy-three and somewhat regal. His name was Vito and the proud Sicilian drove a pristine Cadillac and sported a flashy pinky ring.

What he wasn't was mafioso.

As he slid out of the barber's chair after his weekly shave and haircut, a thunderous crash sent glass everywhere. The old Chevy flew into the shop and pinned the recently-occupied barber's chair against the wall—the confused driver still behind the wheel.

Once the crash victim had been taken away, Vito generously tipped the barber.

"That was a—

"Don't say it, Vito," said the barber. "Please."

"A close shave."

PROMPT:
Polymath

Goldilocks Redux

They were always talking business—even at wedding receptions. Today was no exception.

"Lemme fill you in on who's who," Dominic told Junior, the new kid.

"Those three at the bar? You got Niko Nickels, Danny Dimes, and Kenny Quarters. Nickels is kind of a brainiac. He knows a little bit about lots of stuff. Quarters is way smarter, but only about a few things. And Dimes—"

"Don't tell me," Junior interrupted. "He knows the right amount about everything."

"Nah. He's dumb as a box of rocks. Needs a dime so he can phone a friend to get his own address."

PROMPT:

Resort town

The Choices We Make

"Welcome to Dream Lake." The sign above the dilapidated motel swung in the wind, clearly on its last legs. From the empty parking lot, I leaned against my car and weighed the odds. "This is either the best kept secret for a hundred miles," I offered up, "or—"

"—Or we'll get chain-sawed in our sleep," Jazmyne jumped in.

She nudged me aside and entered the office. She had balls. I'll give her that.

Through the window, I saw the clerk hit a button on the desk.

The door locked.

"Bad news," the clerk drawled. "We're not the best kept secret."

PROMPT:

Amnesia

The Interrogation Room—
Where Memories Go to Die

"Just to recap," Detective Mertens asked, "you don't remember pitching a knife into the sewer or using somebody else's credit card last night, right?"

"I guess not." Stella shrugged.

"Her memory's non-existent," Detective Thorne observed.

"I remember the lady running with a two-piece, forest green, midi dress, with jade Versace hoop earrings and a white Lulu summer hat with a sea foam brim ribbon."

"That's our victim," Mertens confirmed.

"But you were too high to remember anything else about the night, true?" Thorne asked.

"I don't know nothing about the robbery."

"Who said there was a robbery?" Thorne smiled.

PROMPT:

Morpheme

●

Finally, a Reunion Worth Attending

I've known Lawrence my whole life. Other than morphing from "Larry" after Stanford (which he accidentally drops into every conversation), he hasn't changed.

He's still a jerk who uses S.A.T. words to impress.

Two can play that game.

"These appetizers are prosaic," he says at our high school reunion.

I smile. "Still a zoilist, Lawrence!"

He fakes a smile. No clue that I called him a bitter, baseless critic.

When he stuffs his mouth with jumbo shrimp, I salute.

"Madison High's top rakefire."

He humbly accepts the label of a moocher who won't leave.

These reunions are seriously underrated.

PROMPT:

Olly olly oxen free

■

It's Enough to Make Your Head Hurt

The silence was palpable on the drive home after their counseling session.

Tristan broke first. "We made real progress tonight. I now realize that I'm wrong and you're right."

Delia nodded. "Thanks. I really needed to hear that."

"You're welcome."

"But…You were right. I'm sorry."

Once inside the apartment, things escalated. Hearing shouts of "You're right!," "No —you are!" eventually brought the cops.

After listening to each argument, one cop weighed in. "You're definitely right," he told Tristan.

"Thank you."

Once the cops left, Tristan said, "Wait. Was he right about you being right or me being right about you?"

PROMPT:
Use an animal
character

Horace Pays It Forward

I know squirrels aren't meant to be domesticated, but if ever I was going to try, it would be with Horace.

I've learned how to feed him by hand. I know—not a good idea but…he's unique.

While other squirrels chase away the Jays who have learned to open the feeder, Horace doesn't mind. Today, a one-legged bird was unable to balance while opening the feeder. Horace scampered over. When the bird backed away, Horace grabbed a nut and dropped it to the ground.

The bird picked it up and flew off.

An accident?

Nah. Just Horace being Horace.

PROMPT:

Ineluctable prison

Finally Free

Barry was an accountant who worked for a criminal enterprise. After testifying against them (in exchange for a seriously reduced sentence), he received a text: If we don't get you on the inside, we'll see you when you're out.

Five years later, as he rode away from prison, his bus slowed for an accident blocking the road. Naturally, he sensed it was a trap. He countered his paranoia by using a prison relaxation technique. He slowed his breathing. He remembered his plans to get a puppy when he settled down. He smiled.

That's when the bus blew up.

A puppy—seriously?

PROMPT:

The lost year

He Slept While the World Imploded

Nobody expected him to survive the wreck, but almost a year later, he came out of the coma. When I heard the news, I rushed to the hospital.

"You look great," I lied.

"I feel great," he lied back.

Other than a scraggly beard, he looked the same.

"Eleven months I was out… Crazy."

I nodded, thinking about everything he'd missed.

"I love catching up on news after a long trip. I think this qualifies."

He looked at me, expecting an update.

He needed to hear about the pandemic.

"You didn't miss much," I lied again.

Let someone else tell him.

PROMPT:

Patience

Good Things Come to Those Who Wait

He never physically abused her but the incessant verbal and psychological assaults had scarred her deeply. Even as the abuse increased daily, she remained stoic.

Today's barrage led to the breaking point—literally. She smashed the ceramic teapot over his head and used the largest fragment to slit his throat. The mayhem left her surprisingly satisfied.

Snapping out of her internal fantasy, she poured his tranquilized coffee, left the kitchen and texted, "He just drank it."

In an hour, she'd be at her book club, he'd be fast asleep and the arsonist she hired would have the entire house fully engulfed.

PROMPT:

Aridly sarcastic

●

They Put the "ass" in Passionate

From the moment they met, Glen and Lacey were on the same wave length. As they celebrated their tenth anniversary, their shared brain was on full display.

"That was quite a meal, Lace," Glen smiled. "They said the recipe was 'foolproof' but you showed them."

"Thanks, hon. Imagine how good it might've been if I'd cared," Lacey tossed back.

"To be blessed with brains and a bod is amazing," Glen mused. "It's a gift I wish I could share with you."

"Stop it. Your humility's exciting me," she whispered.

They grabbed each other and kissed passionately.

Unconventional? Perhaps. True love? Absolutely.

PROMPT:

Gyhll

Not All Boy Scout Leaders Are Alike

Sporting 100% Boy Scout attire, including official knee socks and shorts, Mr. Kooser (AKA: Mr. Loser) led his troop along the stream. "Compass time, fellas."

Suddenly their path was blocked by three terrifying bikers, their bearded leader inches from Kooser's face.

"Nice shorts, lady." He waved a switchblade.

Kooser surprised him with a Will Smith slap and ran off, shrieking, "Run, boys!" with the bikers close behind.

Stunned, the Scouts cautiously followed.

When they caught up, they found the hairy biker, seriously dead, an official scout knife in his throat.

"Holy crap," one of the Scouts said. "Kooser's definitely no loser."

PROMPT:

Prerequisite

A Touch of Class

Lawrence had been a fixture on the university campus for years. He knew he'd eventually find himself, but for now his routine (and his secret) was that every day began the same way, with a bowl of cereal—and a line of methamphetamine.

Only after he was sufficiently high, could he face another day, and while his habit wasn't as expensive as heroin, he was often forced to steal to keep himself going. This afternoon was going to be one of those days and he dreaded what lay ahead.

He pushed the thought aside, took the podium and began his lecture.

PROMPT:

*Honk if you've never
seen gunfire from a car*

●

Here's What I'm Gonna Do to You

"Even after I tell you I'm gonna bust your nose, you won't be able to stop it—I'm that fast," Nick warned the pushy bar customer.

"After that, I head-butt you. That's my signature move."

A few barstools away, Seth whispered to Jordan, "Why tell the other guy his plan? Won't he swing first?"

"They always back down. Nick's intimidating as shit."

The customer raised his hands in surrender, took a step back—and then threw a lightning-quick punch to the nose, followed by a head-butt.

Nick collapsed.

"Never seen that before," Jordan said.

"Neither has Nick, apparently."

PROMPT:

Oddly-impaired morals

Justice Is Served

Walker was the hardest working cop on the Eastside. He was well known by the law-abiding citizens and the local criminals.

"You steal from people on my side of town," Walker loved to say, "you're stealing from me."

The aggressive cop was very popular with local businesses, who wouldn't let him pay for a meal. Regulations prohibiting gratuities? They were for other cops.

Orders, reprimands and suspensions followed. Walker continued to "put the bad guys away" right up until the day he was fired— the day he finally got it: There really is no such thing as a free lunch.

PROMPT:

Star

Close Encounter with a Celebrity

When Stanley exited baggage claim, the quiet furniture salesman was unprepared for the prank his friends had waiting.

Armed with cameras and microphones, they descended upon Stanley. Cameras flashed. "Reporters" hit him with questions about his upcoming movies. A crowd circled him, assuming he was a celebrity.

Once the shock wore off, Stanley played along with fake smiles and "no comments."

As he waited while his friends went to retrieve their cars, a man with a hat and sunglasses approached.

"Don't know who you are, but thanks for the diversion."

Then Brad Pitt removed his glasses, winked and walked away unnoticed.

PROMPT:

Sickening thud

●

Summer Vacation: Last Day Edition

Daryl and his two equally-obnoxious frat brothers were enjoying their last day on Tahiti. Daryl recklessly whipped the rental jeep into a private driveway where the trio bailed out so their leader could knock a coconut out of a tree.

Daryl chucked a rotten coconut up repeatedly, managing to strike his target, but unable to dislodge it.

"Fuck it. I didn't want one anyway."

They jumped back into the jeep and Daryl spun a donut across the lawn. His frat brothers whooped while admiring the damage. That's when they heard the sickening thud as Daryl's karmic coconut crushed his skull.

PROMPT:

Reverse metamorphosis

Some Zebras Shouldn't Be Allowed to Change Their Stripes

The cops referred to him as a sexually violent predator and experts in the field knew that his violent tendencies would only get worse—eventually leading to murder. They were right.

After committing his third homicide, he got bored. What if he did what the experts said people like him never do? What if he decreased his violent tendencies?

The Internet taught him that lower level crimes didn't get nearly the attention he'd been getting. His new plan: Go back to breaking into houses just to prowl around. He could do this forever and they'd never catch him.

He was right.

PROMPT:

See first, think later

●

So Much for My Suggestion

We're about to enter the company Christmas party. Since I couldn't figure out how to bring it up during the drive, I'll do it now.

"You'll meet the boss tonight," I tell Nick. "Maybe don't say the first thing that pops into your head."

"I got your back," he assures me.

Naturally, Jackye, our transgender CEO, is right there to greet us.

"Jackye, this is my boyfriend, Mick."

They shake hands.

"Woah," Mick backs up. "Big hands. You a dude?"

Jackye turns to me and laughs. "He's everything you said he'd be, bless his heart."

We might survive this after all.

PROMPT:
The boundary between
chaos and calm

He's Testing My Optimism

"Listen up, men." And with that last word, the oblivious sergeant just alienated at least 30 percent of the cops in the briefing room. Please, I pray to the cop gods, not another one of those "us against them" speeches.

Guess I didn't pray hard enough. More about the thin blue line, how we're society's antidote to anarchy (wonder where he found that one).

As I look around the room and take in all the fresh faces, I try to ascertain which ones are buying this shit and which ones know what time it is.

They'll figure it out, I hope.

PROMPT:

Errant

Neither Safe nor Sane

Every Fourth of July was a nightmare for the Becker family. They had the misfortune of living directly behind the Randolphs, raging pyros with an unquenchable thirst for "blowing shit up."

Over the years, random rockets had damaged the roof, car and garden belonging to the Beckers. Without witnesses, the cops said they could do nothing.

Seeking revenge for their parents, the Becker twins staged a strategic fireworks assault. Commercial-grade rockets landed on the Randolph's roof and blasted through garage windows.

Because there were no witnesses, the cops were helpless.

After that, the Randolphs took a pass on the Fourth.

PROMPT:

Craptious overkill

Nobody Knows Killers
Like a Profiler

Detectives Silver and Black (affectionately called "The Raiders" by other cops in the precinct), exited the interrogation room where they were met by FBI profiler Wellington.

"Did you catch his confession?" Silver asked Wellington.

"Just missed it," she said. "But the autopsy report said 14 stab wounds to the face and chest and 12 in the back. That makes it personal. The intense rage indicates a bad relationship between the suspect and victim."

"Actually," Black added, "he said he tried several apartments before finding an open door. Then he just did what the voices told him."

"Fuckin' unpredictable psychopaths," Wellington whined.

PROMPT:

Scorched

Follow Me Where I go

Every time the surveillance team was out on a job, you could always count on one thing—Frankie would jump on the radio. "I've been burned. The target just looked at me hard." And with that, Frankie would pull off of the surveillance because he "knew" that whoever we were tailing had made him as a cop.

He never got burned—he was just paranoid.

Ironically, his paranoia was justified because after he was busted for selling dope, he told the Feds that he never saw them tailing him.

"You guys were good," were his last words as a free man.

PROMPT:

Tempered radicalism

●

Still Fighting the Good Fight

In the 1970s, a domestic terrorist group called the Weather Underground wreaked havoc on government institutions. Several members went to prison, including Bonnie, a fiercely committed leftist.

While her retirement community neighbors called her a radical, they were clueless about her past. She liked it that way.

"Everybody's losing their shit over the new 75-inch TV in the social room," Bonnie said at dinner. "Opiate of the masses."

"You still mad about them locking the doors after 8?" one resident asked.

"A hunger strike would end this oppression—or maybe just a dessert strike," Bonnie offered.

"The cheesecake sucks anyway."

PROMPT:

Execution of an
innocent person

■

Unfortunately, not
Everybody's a Baseball Fan

Holding hands and clearly in love, Dirk and Jessica strolled the deserted downtown street.

Jessica playfully kissed his ear as she removed the .22 revolver from her purse.

Two apartments ahead, a man in a Phillies ball cap exited and strode past.

Jessica whipped around and fired a bullet into the man's brain.

"What're you doing?" Dirk barked.

"Orders were to take out the dude in the Pirates hat," she explained.

"Right, but he's wearing a Phillies hat!"

"It had a 'P' on it," Jessica protested.

"They're not even in the same division," Dirk scowled.

"Like I'm supposed to know that?"

PROMPT:
*Randomly-generated
dog*

The Unpredictable Nature of Online Dating

Moira stood in Edward's lab, marveling at the cages filled with creatures she'd never seen.

"After I read your online profile about working with animals, I was intrigued," she said. "What exactly do you do?"

"Animal species reengineering."

She pointed to a Labrador in a cage. "Is that a prehensile tail?"

"Cool, right? He hangs like a monkey."

"But with that horn, he looks like a rhino."

"Yeah. Still working on that part. At least we found a way to reduce his lethal venom."

She paled.

"You OK?" He flicked his snake-like tongue.

Moira fainted.

Good bone structure, he thought.

PROMPT:

Conundrum

●

Something New on the Menu

It was dinner time, and Laurel and Hardy, two hungry lions, were in a quandary as they studied the dinner menu from afar.

"If we go for the calf, it's an easy catch but a small portion," Laurel noted.

"True, but baby antelope is de-lish," Hardy countered. "Or, we grab the old guy. More meat but tougher."

Fifty yards away, safe in their rented tower, two hunters discussed who to kill: Laurel or Hardy.

BOOM! Lightning exploded the tower, dropping the critically burned hunters to the ground.

Laurel and Hardy, always adaptable, passed on the antelope and opted for barbecue.

PROMPT:

Sweet perturbation

●

Dad's Secret Sweet Spot

Monica's eyes spotted the Broadway Donuts box that Rick placed on the kitchen counter.

"Hands off," Rick said. "I got Dad's favorites before they close for good tomorrow. Ridiculous chocolate croissants."

"That's so sweet," Monica beamed.

"I know. All that sugar."

"Poor Dad'll be crushed. He goes there every Sunday."

Before Rick answered, Bernie entered, spotted the donut box.

"Bad news, Dad. Your croissant place is closing."

Bernie grimaced. "Never liked those things. Way too sweet."

"I thought you loved —"

"Phyllis—the baker with the big bazoombas—she thought I liked 'em so I always got one. Gonna miss that gal."

PROMPT:
Sthenic

Priming the Pump

"Can I have more cereal?" Jaxon asked his daddy.

Drew filled Jaxon's bowl with Sugary Coco Flakes.

"How about chocolate milk with this round?"

Jaxon beamed. "OK!"

Drew turned when Jill cleared her throat.

"Special treat," Drew explained.

Jaxon climbed onto the counter and grabbed a brownie. Looked at Drew for permission.

"Go for it!"

Ten minutes later, Jaxon ran full-speed down the hall.

"Hey!" Drew yelled.

He handed Jaxon a Coke. "Here—stay hydrated."

"When's the ex coming to pick him up for the weekend?" Jill asked.

Drew looked at his watch.

"In about twenty more grams of sugar."

PROMPT:

Tropic of Stupid

Just Hope It's not Contagious

The cops called it "Dumb Ass Drive" because everyone who lived there—at least the school kids and gang bangers—were documented morons. Theories abounded as to the cause: tainted water, generations of head injuries from street fights, a factory spewing toxins…Nobody knew the reason but everybody knew the street's reputation.

Even the smart kids one block over made fun of them by modifying the street sign from "Slow: Children Crossing" to "Slow Children Crossing." You'd think the Dumb Ass Drive Gang would pummel the smart kids for ridiculing them.

They would have — if someone had just explained the joke.

Legend

Legends often include mysteries.
Can you solve the mystery of this legend?

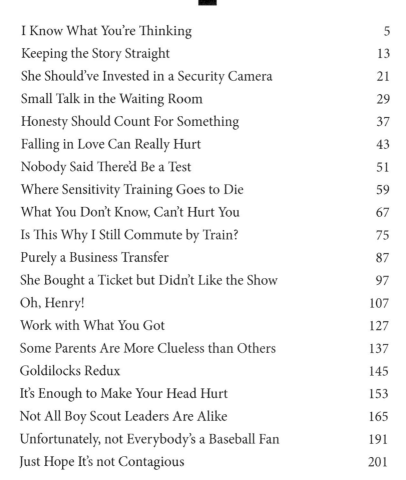

●

The End of the Beginning

Thanks for the read. If you enjoyed it, here's where I get to tell you that *Fast Fiction, Vol. 2* is on the horizon. If not, why are you still reading?

Because I'm on an endless quest for inspiration (in the form of interesting story prompts), if you'd like to contribute, I would absolutely LOVE to hear from you. If I use one of your prompts for inspiration, I'm happy to give you the credit. Feel free to send prompts to:

ScottyCornfieldWriter@gmail.com

In the meantime, if you'd like to stay in the 101-word loop, the best way is to sign up for my blog:

www.scottycornfield.com

I'll send you free stories and updates on what I'm up to. What I won't send you is spam.

That's enough with the self-promotion. Time to get back to writing more of these sprawling sagas…

You can also find me at:

Facebook:
@Scotty.Cornfield.Writer

Twitter:
@ScottyCornfield